Clayton's River Adventure:
Frankfort to Boonesborough

—— by ——

Linda M. Penn & Frank J. Feger

Illustrated by Melissa Quinio

Printed in the United States of America

First Printing, 2016

ISBN 978-0-9908807-0-7

Racing to Joy Press
P.O. Box 654
Crestwood, KY 40031

www.LindaMPenn.com/Racing-To-Joy-Press.html

Acknowledgements

To God, thanks for bringing another book together with us. There have been instances where thoughts just seemed to "come out of nowhere," but we know they came from You.

To our families and friends, thanks for the support.

To the teachers, parents, and others that we have talked with at book signings and presentations, thanks for your kind comments and ideas. We have incorporated some of your ideas into this book.

To Marie, Layout Designer and Editor, thanks for your loyalty and continued support on the Clayton projects. And to Melissa, our Illustrator, whose creations bring our book to life!

To all the children who will read this book – Happy Reading!

Sincerely,
Frank and Linda

Table of Contents

Chapter 1
Clayton Meets Daisy

Clayton and his friend, Austin, along with Clayton's Mom and Grampy thanked Governor and First Lady Beshear again for the candy and tour of the candy factory.

"And thank you for making us Kentucky Colonels," Clayton added.

"You're welcome. It has been delightful to meet you, your friend, and your family," Mr. Beshear said.

"We do not have anything on our schedules for the remainder of the day," Mrs. Beshear said. "Would you like to take a ride in our limo and tour the Governor's Mansion?"

"Yes, yes! Never been in a limo," Austin said with enthusiasm. "Grampy, do we have time before we shove off?"

"Oh, I think so, I have never been in a limo either!"

"Me either," Mom said. "And I would love to see the Mansion!"

"Well, include me!" Clayton pointed to himself.

After they all climbed into the limo and buckled up, Clayton commented, "So many seats in here, it is so big in here, reminds me of a movie theater."

At the Governor's Mansion, the group followed the Beshears and began their tour.

"We will be leaving here in a few months because a new governor is being elected in November," Mrs. Beshear said.

Just then, as they entered the kitchen, from around the corner, the group heard scratching on the tile floor. Out bounded a small, black and tan beagle hound right into Clayton's arm as he bent down to pet the dog. Austin bent down too and the dog licked both of the boys, and wagged its tail furiously.

"Boys, it appears that Daisy really likes you," Mr. Beshear said. "We won't be able to take her with us when we move back to Winchester. We have been keeping her for the Frankfort Humane Society for about a month."

"Do you have a dog, Clayton and Austin?" Mrs. Beshear asked. "We have been concerned about finding a good home for her. Obviously, Daisy is really bonding with you two. Would either of you like to be her permanent owner?"

"I don't have a dog now," Clayton responded. "We did have a dog but she died about a year ago."

"I already have a dog at home," Austin said, "but I would love to play with Daisy when I come over to your house, Clayton."

"I would love to be Daisy's owner," Clayton smiled. "Grampy?"

"Well…" Grampy tilted his head back and forth and looked at Mom pensively.

"Do I have to be the one to make the decision?" Mom asked as Clayton, Austin, Grampy, and the Beshears stared at her.

"I really like Daisy too," Mom stammered as Daisy also looked at Mom and continued wagging her tail. "I have questions, however. How do we keep a dog on a boat? What kind of dogfood? Where does she go to the bathroom? Who is going to be responsible for her daily needs? Where will she sleep? Has she been spayed?"

"We have dog bowls, dogfood, treats, a leash, and a few toys," Mr. Beshear offered.

"And she has been spayed and is up to date on her

doggie shots," Mrs. Beshear told Mom. "You might want to purchase a doggie bed. She has been sleeping on a rug beside my bed."

"And we will notify the Humane Society about a permanent owner," Mr. Beshear said.

"I saw a pet shop about a block from the marina," Grampy hopefully continued to look at Mom. "You know what? Your Granny Rose and I brought a poodle named Anja home from Germany years ago. Well, we sorta did – the airline lost Anja in her cage and they found her in Boston, not New York City where I landed. I think your Granny Rose would be happy if Clayton had another dog."

"Okay, sounds like you have acquired a new dog!" Mom said cheerfully as the group did their fist bumps and then reached down to pet Daisy. "I'm sure your dad will approve if you agree to be responsible for Daisy."

"Alright!" Clayton pumped his arms and then gave Daisy a big hug. Daisy seemed to voice her approval also as she gave Clayton more licks on his face.

"You will have all of Daisy's belongings to carry to the boat. We could get our limo driver to take you and Daisy there. If you have any extra time before you head back to Louisville, I would suggest you proceed on down the Kentucky River to Boonesborough. They are having a

Coonskin Cap Festival there. You could even go on further to Beattyville where the Kentucky River begins. That town has a Wooly Worm Festival.

"Sounds like fun," Grampy clapped his hands. "Are you in, Mom, Clayton, and Austin?"

"You will need to call your parents, Austin, and also call your Dad, Clayton," Mom said as she handed the cell phone to Austin.

"YES, YES, YES! THEY SAID YES" Austin did the "quarterback making a touchdown" dance.

Clayton and Mom called his Dad. "Guess what?" Clayton said dejectedly with a frown on his face. "JUST KIDDING! DAD SAID YES!!!!!" Clayton yelled as he did the "touchdown" dance also. "More adventuring and meandering on the Kentucky River!"

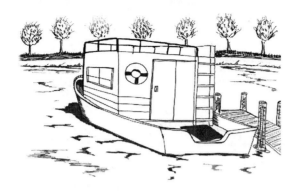

Chapter 2
The Wee Wee Mat

As the Beshears said their good-byes to Daisy and helped the group get Daisy's supplies into the limo, Clayton shook hands with the Beshears and promised to take good care of Daisy.

"Here is our personal cell phone number. Give us a call when you and Daisy get settled in her new home," Mrs. Beshear said.

As the limo pulled up to the Frankfort Boat Club Marina, Austin and Mom led Daisy onboard the *Granny Rose* while Grampy and Clayton walked to the pet shop.

"May I suggest a wee-wee mat for your dog to use on the boat?" Mr. Manning at the pet shop said. "And here is a comfortable doggie bed, a medium size should work fine for a beagle dog."

"We can put the wee-wee mat at the back of the boat on the flat motor cover area," Grampy said. "We'll put the doggie bed in your room, Clayton."

"Sure thing. Grampy, can we get some more toys for Daisy? Maybe some rawhide sticks?"

"Good idea, Clayton," Grampy answered.

After their purchases, Clayton and Grampy headed back to the boat. They found Mom and Austin giving Daisy a tour of the *Granny Rose*.

"Daisy, look what we got for you! A wee-wee mat!" Clayton laughed as he led Daisy to the back of the boat where he placed the mat.

"Grampy! Mom! Austin! It works! Daisy understands what to do on this mat!" Clayton exclaimed as he proudly brought Daisy back to the kitchen area. They fed Daisy and filled her water bowl.

"Smart dog, don't you think?" Clayton continued to pet Daisy.

"Awesome," Austin responded.

"Okay, you deckhands, let's look at our checklist to make sure we are ready to depart in the morning. The boys checked the water level gauge and made sure the holding tank had been emptied. Grampy checked the gas gauge. Mom checked the food supplies.

"After we grill our hamburgers for dinner, I will need to stock up on more meat, fruit, veggies, and bread, and of course, some ice cream, at the marina store.

"I'll go with you," Grampy said, "and I'll pay our dock fee. At $3.00 a foot, that totals $126.00 because the *Granny Rose* is 42 feet in length. And we have docked here two days, so the grand total will be $252.00."

Mom, Grampy, and Austin grilled the burgers while Clayton set the table.

After their dinner and the trip to the marina store, Grampy yawned, "Troops, it's about that time. Let's get to bed so we can get an early start in the morning for Boonesborough."

"Okay, come on Daisy!" Clayton motioned to Daisy. "Let's go to the wee-wee mat. And then let's get you settled in your brand new bed! You are going to love the cruising on the river tomorrow."

— Chapter 3 —
Meeting Camryn and Rocco

Clayton and Austin were sleeping on, even as the sun rose. Daisy began to move around in her bed and jumped up on Clayton's bed, licking him in the face. She began barking and appeared to be alarmed at something outside. She ran to the steps to go to the upper deck and continued to beckon Clayton to follow her.

"Okay, girl, let's go to the wee-wee mat," Clayton said as he attached the leash to Daisy's collar.

"What's the matter?" Clayton asked as Daisy kept barking and running to the railing of the *Granny Rose*, even after using the wee-wee mat. "Let's go check it out."

Clayton and Daisy walked along the deck of the marina with Daisy pulling on the leash. There in front of them was an elderly gentleman and a young girl walking a cute, little, black poodle dog.

"Good morning, sir," Clayton said as the dogs greeted each other by licking and sniffing.

"Good morning, young man, looks like you have a good guard dog there."

"Yes, my family and I just got her yesterday. We are still getting accustomed to each other. This is Daisy."

"Nice dog," the girl said. "May I pet her?"

"Sure, what is your dog's name? And your name? My name is Clayton."

"This is Rocco, and I'm Camryn and here is Grandpa Logan," she said as she pointed to the older man. Nice to meet you, Clayton. We are going to the Daniel Boone gravesite and then we're off for Boonesborough and the Coonskin Cap Festival."

"Yes! My Grampy, Mom, and my friend, Austin, are headed there to the festival and also to Shaker Village!" Clayton grinned. "Maybe we will see you there." Clayton shook hands with Grandpa Logan, Camryn, and Rocco. "It was fun meeting you."

"Safe travels," Grandpa Logan said as he and Clayton guided their dogs to their respective houseboats.

"Man, what took you so long?" Austin asked as Clayton and Daisy returned to the *Granny Rose*. "Grampy is anxious to get going."

"Met another Grampy," Clayton explained to Austin. His granddaughter is Camryn and their dog is Rocco. Found out they are going to the Daniel Boone gravesite and on to the Coonskin Cap Festival too."

"Okay, time to depart. We've been in Frankfort long enough. We need to get going on our journey to Boonesborough," Grampy said. "We are at mile marker 65 and we will conclude at marker 176, about 110 miles."

Got a math problem for you fellows," Mom said. We will travel about 10 miles an hour on the Kentucky River, so, how long will it take us to get to Boonesborough?"

"I'll think on that, and get back with you," Austin contemplated as he and Clayton untied the ropes and stored the bumpers."

"Generator operating, engines started," Grampy declared, backing the *Granny Rose* from the marina slip and making the turn south on the Kentucky.

"Look up at the top of that hill," Mom said. "That is the gravesite and monument dedicated to Daniel Boone and Rebecca, his wife.

"Grampy, I know we need to get on down the river, but could we tie up to a pier up ahead and briefly visit the site?" Clayton asked with a hopeful look on his face.

"We promise it won't take over 15 minutes! Right, fellows?" Mom peered at Clayton and Austin.

"YES!" exclaimed Clayton and Austin.

"Alright," Grampy agreed. "Daniel Boone is a very famous and important person in the history of the settlement of Kentucky. Maybe you guys could research on the iPad about Boonesborough when we are cruising along on the Kentucky River."

"Wow, what a view of Frankfort from up here." Austin beamed as they all reached the hilltop. "Look, there is the new Capitol building."

"And I see the lock number 4 that we traveled through on the Kentucky River," chimed in Clayton. "Thanks, Grampy, for allowing us to stop here."

"You are welcome. I'm glad to see this monument to Mr. Boone," Grampy answered as he snapped pictures of everyone. "We will journey through lock number 5 about 20 more miles down the river, at mile marker 82."

As the group made their way back down the hill to the *Granny Rose*, Mom suggested to the boys they research also about Woodford County and the horse farms located there. "We will be traveling through Woodford County very soon on the river. We will be close to the City of Versailles."

"Grampy, did you tell me once that you and my

Granny Rose owned a horse?" Clayton asked.

Chapter 4
Woodford County:
'Horse Capital Of The World'

"Yes, we did," Grampy answered. We bought a yearling foal at the Keeneland Spring Sales. It was a filly and her name was Sweikart Miss. She was born in Woodford County – the 'horse capital of the world.' Her trainer, Mr. McGee, had high hopes for the horse's racing career during the three years we owned her. Did you notice her horseshoe hanging over the doorway to my bedroom?"

"No, I didn't but I'll check it out," Austin nodded. "So why did you keep a horseshoe?"

"Horses wear out their shoes just like us," Grampy said as he lifted up his shoe to show its sole. The more horses run, the quicker their shoes need replacing. Rose and I kept the horseshoe as a way to remember our fun times with the horse."

"How many races did you win?" inquired Clayton.

"She won two races. Wow, we had big dreams of us being in the Winners' Circle at Churchill Downs in Louisville for the Kentucky Derby, the most famous horse race for three year old horses. Only about 20 horses out of the 8,000 registered thoroughbred foals in the United States each year make it to the Kentucky Derby."

"Another Math problem for you fellows!" Mom laughed. "What percentage make it to the track for the Derby?"

"Okay, I'll think on that problem too and get back with you," Austin grinned.

"I remember going to the stables to visit Sweikart Miss," Mom said. "Your Aunts Amy, Jennifer, and Sara and I would feed the horse carrots and we wanted to bring the horse home with us and put her in our backyard. We thought she was lonely in the stable by herself and we cried when we had to leave her there."

"Grampy, how much money did you win?" Clayton rubbed his fingers together as if counting dollar bills.

"Some," Grampy smiled. "Honestly, your Granny Rose and I were into racing the horse for enjoyment. It was our hobby and we met interesting people in our racing adventures. I am still friends with many of them. We learned a great deal about horses, especially from Trainer McGee."

"What happened to your horse?" Austin asked.

Grampy had a sad looking face and hesitated about answering that question. "Well...she ran well in the beginning...for about the first eight months. Rose and I were so excited to get those trophies. We loved that horse," Grampy appeared to be getting choked up.

"But she began to lose races, coming in third, fourth, or worse," Grampy continued as his shoulders slumped and his head bent down. "Horses are rated by their wins and losses and if their ratings slip down too much, the horses have to be placed in a claiming race. Since Sweikart Miss's ratings dropped, Rose, Trainer McGee, and I had no choice but to run her in a claiming race. Another horse enthusiast claimed Sweikart Miss, paid us the $20,000 claiming fee and took her to his stables in hopes she might race better under his direction."

"Mom, did you cry when you lost the horse to another owner?" Clayton asked. "That's a sad story."

"We all cried!" Mom answered.

"What happens to horses when they get too old or they aren't good enough to race anymore?" Austin looked very sad too.

"Most horses are well cared for in their retirement years," Grampy seemed to perk up, sensing the whole group was having a down moment.

"Unfortunately, for whatever reason, some people just turn their animals out into the wild and they become strays," Mom said. "The good news is that the Kentucky Humane Society and the Kentucky Horse Park in Lexington, Kentucky receive money from donors to help take care of the strays. Also, Governor Beshear signed House Bill 312 which provides money to help care for the strays."

"Alright, that is uplifting news," Clayton pumped his fist. "Hopefully, all the retired horses will have nice owners who make sure the horses have lots of hay to eat and salt to lick and they can run in the pastures of blue grass."

"Salt to lick?" Austin exclaimed with a grimace on his face.

Chapter 5
Daisy's Warning Saves Lakota

"Yes, I remember learning from Trainer McGee that salt is very important to a horses's diet," Mom answered. "A horse needs at least two tablespoons of salt per day. If horses don't get enough salt, they may stop eating and not drink enough to stay hydrated. The trainers usually provide blocks of salt near the horses' feeding areas."

"Remember when we tied up at Canes Run Creek, we saw the buffalo trail to Big Bone Lick State Park, the site of salt mounds?" Grampy asked.

"Yes," Clayton answered. "And I remember seeing salt blocks for the cows at Uncle Eugene's farm.

"The Kentucky Humane Society places salt blocks out in the wild for stray horses," Mom added.

"Lock Number 5 coming up," Grampy said. "Austin,

will you use the marine radio, channel 13, and call the Lockmaster for permission to proceed through the lock?"

"Sure thing!" Austin replied.

As Austin made the call, Clayton and Mom removed the bumpers from storage.

"We are good to go!" Austin shouted, "need the bumpers on the port side."

As Grampy guided the *Granny Rose* into the lock, Mom and the boys tied to the left side of the lock.

"Would you boys like to climb the ladder on the side of the lock and come up here to the rim and walk around while your boat is changing water levels in the lock?" the Lockmaster asked.

The boys looked to Grampy and Mom for the okay and they motioned for the boys to go ahead.

"Wow, this is so COOL!" Austin exclaimed as he and Clayton stood on the rim of the lock watching the *Granny Rose* ascend 25 ft. to the new water level.

"Now we are even with the boat and we didn't move at all. It was the water rising in the lock," Clayton said as he took pictures with his iPad.

"Time to step back onto the boat," Grampy called. "On to Mercer County now. We will tie up and eat lunch at Chapman's Bend. It was named for the family who settled in that area in the pioneer days. There are many bends in the Kentucky River and they are named for families who owned and settled property many years ago.

Grampy guided the *Granny Rose* to the fork of the Kentucky River and Wilson's Creek at Chapman's Bend and the boys began to tie ropes to a tree.

Just then, Daisy arose from her normally quiet resting area and barked loudly.

"What is it, Daisy?" Clayton said as Daisy barked continually. "You have been so quiet on this river trip. What's wrong?"

Clayton petted her but she jumped all around and kept running toward the railing on the right side.

"Look over there on the starboard side!" Mom cried out. "There's a horse in the mud close to the shore. It could be a sand bar and the horse might be stuck. Daisy has been trying to warn us about the horse's dilemma."

"Mom, there's a man over there in the open field close to the woods," Clayton shouted.

"I'll blast the horn to get his attention," Grampy said.

"He heard the horn," Austin yelled. "He's coming down here.

"Hello, Sir, " Grampy called. "Is that your horse in the mud?"

"Yes, Lakota, my colt, got loose from her stall when I was feeding her. I have been hunting for her for at least an hour. Thank you for alerting me."

"It was our dog, Daisy, who warned us something was wrong," Grampy said.

"We have some extra ropes to help you get the horse out," Clayton offered.

With a push and pull, and the use of the ropes, the group was able to get the horse free and onto solid footing on the shore.

"Thank you so much, " the man said. " I am William Chapman. Lakota must have come down here to get a drink. If it hadn't been for you, she might have drown. I took her in last week. She was a stray horse just wandering like she was lost."

As Grampy introduced his group, Daisy ran over to Lakota and licked her feet and legs. Lakota responded with a nuzzle to Daisy.

"It's as if Daisy sensed your horse was in trouble and warned us," Austin said as he and Clayton stroked Daisy and Lakota lovingly. "We had been talking about stray horses. How sad! And I was just learning about horses needing salt blocks."

"Yes, so right, and thank you too, Daisy," Mr.

Chapman said as he petted Daisy.

"And I have something for you, good citizens." Mr. Chapman reached in his coat pocket and pulled out a thin hoop with colored yarn strung through it and feathers hanging down.

"Oh, it's a dream-catcher!" Mom smiled.

"I read a story about a little Native American boy from the Lakota tribe and the legend of a dream-catcher," Clayton said. Good dreams passed through the center of the hoop to him when he was asleep and bad dreams were trapped in the web where they died out."

"I would like for you boys to have this dream-catcher and may you have lots of good dreams." Mr. Chapman handed it to the boys.

"Alright, thank you, thank you!" Clayton and Austin shook hands with Mr. Chapman.

"We will hang this above our bunks," Clayton said proudly as he, Austin, and Daisy headed below deck with their reward.

Chapter 6
Youngsters to Young Men

As the boys hung their dream-catcher on the ceiling light above their beds, Clayton touched the center hole of the dream-catcher. "Good dreams, come pass through here tonight."

"Me too!" Austin added. "And I'm dreaming and wishing right now to go fishing again on this Kentucky River adventure!"

They heard Mom call them for lunch and they promptly bounded up the stairs to the kitchen.

"Mr. Chapman, would you like a turkey sandwich for lunch?" Mom asked.

"That would be great," he answered.

Austin nudged Clayton. "Should we ask Grampy if we can stay tied up here and go fishing this afternoon?"

"Good idea," Clayton answered quietly. "Let's go for it!"

"Boys, I overheard your idea," Mr. Chapman whispered back to the boys. I was planning to do some fishing myself at my pond just over the rise. The pond was stocked with bass by the Kentucky Fish and Wildlife Department, so anything we catch could be our dinner. Let's go talk to Grampy."

The boys and Mr. Chapman approached Grampy with big grins. "We have an idea!" Mr. Chapman said. "Would you like to go fishing with me this afternoon at my pond? We could even have a fish fry later for dinner!"

"The pond is right over the hill," Austin added.

"And his pond has been stocked with BASS by the Kentucky Fish and Wildlife Department," Clayton exclaimed. "Yes, BASS!"

"Sounds great to me if your Mom agrees," Grampy answered.

"Sure," Mom agreed. "I have the ingredients onboard that we need for a fish fry. And I am excited that the fish will be coming from your pond, Mr. Chapman. I just recently read an article about water pollution in Kentucky's rivers and there was a warning not to eat fish caught in Kentucky rivers."

"I read that too," Grampy said. "Even with Kentucky's Clean Water Act of 44 years ago, toxic contaminents are still an issue. The runoff from the mountaintop strip mines in eastern Kentucky contain unsafe levels of mercury and sulpher."

"Yes," said Mr. Chapman, "it is best to enjoy fishing in the rivers but then release the fish back into the water. My pond doesn't get any runoff water from creeks or rivers, so the fish would be safe to eat."

After lunch, Grampy, Mom, and the boys gathered their fishing gear and headed up the hill following Mr. Chapman to his pond.

"Come get your bait. I just dug these big, juicy nightcrawlers last night," Mr. Chapman said as he held up a pail full of squiggly worms.

"Look at those creatures!" Clayton exclaimed.

"They look like baby snakes!" Mom screamed.

"These worms don't look like the worms we used when we fished before," Austin remarked.

"No, we bought red worms that day," Grampy said. "You can also use crickets, minnows, waxworms, or even artificial bait.

"But bass love NIGHTCRAWLERS!" Mr. Chapman smiled. "Okay, let's catch dinner."

After a couple of hours of fishing, the group hauled their catch back to the *Granny Rose.*

"Hey, you young fishermen, do you want to learn to fillet a fish?" Mr. Chapman asked as he reached carefully in his tackle box for his fillet knife.

Clayton, Austin, Grampy, and Mom gathered around Mr. Chapman as he began his instructions. He took a bass out of the bucket and placed it firmly on a large flat rock.

"Just behind the dorsal fin of the fish, make a single cut straight down the ribcage to the tail, turn it over, and do the same to the other side of the fish. You have nice, full fillets without bones. Very little cutting and very little mess."

"And plenty of good food," Mom added as she took pictures of Clayton and Austin with their catch.

"Be careful with the knife, guys. It has to be extremely sharp to cut the fish in one single stroke," Grampy cautioned.

Very intently, the boys watched Mr. Chapman and Grampy fillet more fish.

"Your turn now, Clayton and Austin," Grampy said handing the knife to Clayton.

Clayton placed the fish solidly on the rock with his left hand and with his shaking right hand, he followed Mr.

Chapman's directions. Clayton didn't say a word as he completed his job and handed the knife to Austin, who also fixed his attention on the fish and the knife. Looking very intently at the chore ahead of him, Austin hesitated, took a deep breath, and completed the filleting.

"I can't believe I just did that," Clayton pondered. His right hand was still shaking as he let out of huge sigh.

"Me too," Austin said, wiping his forehead that was dripping with sweat. "That was intense."

"So proud of you youngsters," Mom said. "Well, I guess I really can't call you youngsters anymore, you are becoming young men." She gave the boys a pat on their backs.

"That was a real thrill. Can't wait to tell my family what we did when I call them tonight," Austin said as he and Clayton gave the thumbs up to each other.

"Grampy, do you think sometime we could go fishing with you in your bass boat on the lake back home?" Clayton asked. "And fillet the fish for dinner?" Clayton had that hopeful sparkle in his eyes as he looked at Grampy.

"Well...uh...let me think," Grampy stammered. "Of course, sure, that would be a big YES!" Grampy replied, nodding his head is agreement.

After the fish fry and all the good-byes and thank

you's to Mr. Chapman, along with the nightly phone calls to families back in Louisville, Grampy began to yawn. "I am going to turn in now. Tomorrow will be a big day. We will be seeing the high cliffs above the Kentucky River called the Palisades. You youngsters ready to hit the hay?"

Mom gave Grampy an "oh no" look and shook her head.

"Oh, sorry about that 'youngsters' comment, I mean: you 'YOUNG MEN,' are you ready to go to bed?" Grampy grinned.

"Thanks for your confidence in us, Mom and Grampy!" Clayton commented, giving himself and Austin a pat on the back.

As Clayton and Austin slid into their bunks, the last thing Clayton saw was the dream-catcher. "Hey, Austin, look up, I see those good dreams getting ready to go through the dream-catcher tonight?"

Chapter 7
Clayton's Dream

Characters and Places in Clayton's Dream:

Morning Rose – Granny Rose
Running Fox – Austin
Chief Proud Foot – Grampy
Brave Deer – Austin's Dad
Running Bird – Clayton
Little Flower – Austin's Mom

Evening Star – Clayton's Mom
Beautiful River – Ohio River
Running Bear – Clayton's Dad
Little River – Kentucky River
Little White Dove - Camryn

"Evening Star (Mom), we've been on this canoe adventure on the Beautiful River (Ohio River) and then on the Little River (Kentucky River) for a long time. Does Chief Proud Foot (Grampy) know where we are going? When are we going to stop and build a new village?"

"Chief Proud Foot (Grampy) has a plan to resettle our Shawnee tribe in a beautiful high cliff area, the Palisades, along this Little River (Kentucky River)," answered

Evening Star (Mom). "There are caves where we will live, crystal clear waters where we will fish, and woods to hunt deer, elk, fox, buffalo, and rabbits. The caves will warm us in the winter and cool us in the summer and keep us safe from bears and any other predators."

Running Bear (Clayton's Dad), who was in the rear of the canoe doing the guiding, while Running Bird (Clayton) and Evening Star (Mom) were paddling, said, "Be not worried, Running Bird (Clayton), our Chief Proud Foot (Grampy) will lead our tribe into the Palisades. We will search for the best caves to set up our homes."

Just then, Chief Proud Foot (Grampy), who was in the lead canoe with Morning Rose (Granny Rose), turned around and bellowed to the occupants in the following five canoes that the high cliffs were just around the bend in the Little River (Kentucky River). "Our new tribal home!" he shouted.

Daisy barked continuously and moved about Running Bird's (Clayton) canoe as if anticipating something important was about to happen. Running Bird (Clayton) patted her head. "We will be out of this canoe very soon, girl, I promise!"

"I see a safe place to land our canoes," Brave Deer (Austin's Dad) exclaimed to Little Flower (Austin's Mom) and Running Fox (Austin), who were in the third canoe. Running Fox (Austin) called back to the other canoes' occupants and pointed to the cliffs and landing area ahead.

After all the tribe members disembarked from their canoes, Chief Proud Foot (Grampy) proudly lifted his hands high up to the sky. "I declare this to be called Shawnee Landing and these caves are to be known as Shawnee Village."

As Chief Proud Foot (Grampy) and Morning Rose (Granny Rose) began searching the area for the best caves to use as homes, other Shawnee tribe members began unloading the canoes. Brave Deer (Austin's Dad) and Running Bear (Clayton's Dad) followed Chief Proud Foot (Grampy) and Morning Rose (Granny Rose) and checked the caves for bears or any other signs of danger.

"Hey, Running Fox (Austin)," hollered Running Bird (Clayton), "let's grab our bows and arrows and hunt for dinner."

"I'm with you!" Running Fox (Austin) exclaimed. "Look at those cliffs, like steps to the sky!"

"Awesome!" Running Bird (Clayton) shouted while looking upward. "We need to go find dinner...like...NOW," he said while rubbing his stomach.

The boys headed off to the woods and Chief Proud

Foot (Grampy) hollered to the others, "I found a huge cave with a natural chimney opening."

With a grand shout of happiness, Morning Rose (Granny Rose) held her hands skyward. "This cave is perfect for cooking!"

As the other tribe members located other nearby caves and continued the search for any unwanted inhabitants in them, Little Flower (Austin's Mom) and Evening Star (Mom) combed the area for wild berries.

Later that afternoon, upon the return of Running Bird (Clayton) and Running Fox (Austin) with several rabbits, the boys informed Chief Proud Foot (Grampy) they had seen a group of wild horses.

"That is good news," the chief said. "We need horses for traveling and also to help us do work in the fields.

"We also have good news," said Little Flower (Austin's Mom). Evening Star (Mom) and I picked a bunch of wild berries. And we saw honeysuckle and herbs for our medicines, like garlic and mustard and onions.

"Gather together, Shawnee tribe. Let's give praise for our beautiful and safe cave homes, the plentiful wildlife, fish, berries, and herbs," Chief Proud Foot (Grampy) professed. "We will live here and have happy lives for years to come."

As nightfall came and the sun set behind the cliffs, Running Bird (Clayton) removed his arrowhead and bear tooth necklace from his neck. He had a strong feeling that was urging him to bury it in the soil next to the opening of his new tribal cave home to protect the tribe from harm.

Chapter 8
Stairways to Heaven

"Let's get rollin' down the river," Grampy sang to the boys below deck. "The sun is up! Next stop, the Palisades."

Austin bounded out of his bed, got dressed, and raced up the steps to the main deck while Daisy licked Clayton all over his face, as if to say "Time is wasting!"

"Daisy, you were in my dream last night," Clayton said, yawning. He looked up at the dream-catcher. "It was a good dream. Okay, let's go, next up, wee-wee mat. I can't wait to tell everyone about the dream."

"Clayton, how did you sleep? Are you ready for breakfast?" Mom asked as Clayton lumbered up the steps, taking Daisy to the wee-wee mat and filling her bowls with food and clean water.

"I slept really weird. My arms are tired from rowing

a canoe for a couple of months with a Shawnee tribe. Actually, we were all members of the tribe." Clayton rubbed his arms and shoulders.

"What do you mean?" Grampy questioned.

"You were Chief Proud Foot," Clayton answered. "I was Running Bird. Granny Rose was even in the dream. She was named Morning Rose. You were there too, Mom, I mean Evening Star. Dad's name was Running Bear. We were all in the lead canoe."

"Wow, where did you get those names?" Austin laughed. "So, was I in the dream too? Was I some kind of Running something?"

"Oh, yes," Clayton nodded. You were Running Fox and you and your mom and dad were in the canoe behind ours. Your mom was Little Flower and your dad was Brave Deer. Remember Camryn, her Grandpa, and little Rocco? They were all in the third canoe. Camryn was Little White Dove."

"Okay," Mom said cautiously. "So what were we all doing, just out rowing for fun? Or were we headed somewhere special?"

"There were six canoes filled with people, and we were all on the Kentucky River traveling to new homes in the caves of the Palisades with Chief Proud Foot leading the way," Clayton said proudly, bowing to Grampy.

"Well, Chief Proud Foot says that it is time to finish eating and head out."

While everyone enjoyed their bacon and eggs, Clayton rambled on about his dream.

"Running Fox, you and I had to shoot our bows and arrows to get rabbits for our dinner," Clayton said, pretending to shoot a rabbit. "Boing!"

"Hey, man, I sure am glad that we didn't have to shoot our breakfast today," Austin said.

"Guess what, Mom? You and Austin's mom had to pick wild berries for the tribe."

"Funny, I don't have any scratches on my fingers or arms," Mom laughed.

"What a dream," Grampy said, "I guess that dream-catcher really did its job."

"So, did your dream-catcher only allow good dreams to travel through it?" Mom asked with a concerned smile.

"Oh, yes, and I even buried an arrowhead and bear tooth necklace to keep the tribe safe," Clayton announced.

"Let's go find that ancestral home of ours, Clayton," Grampy said, as he and the boys untied the ropes and stored them away. Mom secured everything in the kitchen area.

"Soon we will begin seeing the STAIRWAYS TO HEAVEN," Grampy declared, as he started the engines of the *Granny Rose.*

As they made their way down the river, Grampy looked over the Kentucky River map at the wheelhouse station.

"The Shawnee Run and Sand Bar are about five miles from here. There really was a tribe of Shawnee that lived in this area before the European settlers explored here. Captain James Harrod and his followers met many of the tribes as he and the other explorers settled all along the Kentucky and the Ohio Rivers. Some native tribes welcomed them but others felt threatened, afraid the new settlers would take away their land.

"Grampy, could we...well, I know we need to get on to Boonesborough, but could we... tie up at Shawnee Run and explore, well...maybe for just a little while?" Clayton stammered.

"Sure," Grampy answered. "Do you think we will find any remnants of the Shawnee Village where we all were last night in your dream?" Grampy, Mom, and Austin laughed, but Clayton just grimaced.

The group traveled on down the river, waving to the families who were fishing and grilling at the shore's edge.

They passed other houseboats whose occupants asked, "Hey, where are you all headed?"

"Boonesborough, the Coonskin Cap Festival!" Clayton and Austin yelled back.

Clayton and Austin kept looking skyward for big cliffs, and they researched on the iPad about Daniel Boone and Boonesborough, taking notes in their journals.

"Hey, everybody, look up there!" Austin exclaimed. "Those rocks look like chimneys!"

"And there are trees growing right out of the rocks!" Clayton shouted. He pointed to large clumps of green spread out from the rugged white layers of rocks.

"The Palisades! And I see the Shawnee Landing area ahead," Grampy called. "Let's prepare to tie up the long ropes from the back of the boat to the trees. We will need to use the ladder at the front to disembark. I'll bring some flashlights in case we explore in some caves."

The group steadied themselves moving down the ladder and planted their feet securely along the shore.

"Chief Proud Foot declares this is Shawnee Landing. We have returned." Grampy boasted. He spread his arms wide with his hands up to the sky.

"Let's explore!" Clayton motioned to the others to follow him.

Chapter 9
The Necklace

Clayton led the way to the clearing where he thought the tribal cave home was located.

"Let's dig for some arrowheads while we are here," Austin suggested.

"YES!" exclaimed Clayton. "Come on Daisy, you can help us."

Clayton, Austin and Daisy poked into the earth but their search turned up empty.

"Look over there! See those trees," Clayton said. "Just like in my dream."

The tree line and cave entrances were laid out in such a way that it was obvious where a Native American tribe would have resided in the main cave.

"Mom, see that pit? Granny Rose cooked the rabbits

over a pit like that in my dream. They were hanging over a fire from long, sharp rods. And up there is a chimney opening where the smoke from a fire went out of the cave."

"Was all that in your dream?" Mom questioned. "Those are some very interesting details for you to remember."

"Yes, and my bed was right here," Clayton laid down in the soft soil in the right corner of the main room of the cave. Daisy promptly climbed on top of Clayton and began licking his face.

"And there is a natural spring that oozed up into the cave where water came into the cave for them to use," Clayton added, directing the others to look at the tiny stream of water coming from the opening in the earth.

"BONES! OVER HERE!" Austin yelled as he scratched up the surface of the soil in the left corner of the room.

"Probably from deer or elk," Grampy surmised.

"Any rabbit bones? After all, we shot a whole bunch of them," Clayton laughed as he and Daisy got up from their bed to investigate the finds in the soil. Daisy opened her mouth to pick up a bone but after sniffing it, decided to leave it be.

"Let's explore further in the cave," Grampy called

after the boys finished their bone research. "Maybe we can find more evidence of the Native American tribes. Here, everyone take a flashlight."

Proceeding slowly in the dark with only the four flashlights in their shaky hands, they came upon some colors on the wall.

"Check this out," Clayton called. "Shine the flashlights over here."

"Looks like a painting of two Native American boys holding up rabbits, " Grampy beamed. "I can't believe it, but that looks like my Rose starting a fire with cattails at the pit."

"And that looks like you, Grampy, skinning a rabbit!" Austin cheered. "This is just too much! Are you guys sure you haven't been here before?" Austin continued to shake his head and his face showed disbelief.

"Honest, my dream was just like this," Clayton said emphatically.

"Yes, yes, Clayton," Mom said calmly, "not sure how this all happened, but we believe you had the dream."

Daisy began barking, turning around in circles, and urging the group back to the entrance and out of this area.

"Maybe we should get back to the sunlight now," Grampy said, shaking his head also.

As the group exited the cave, all of them still anxious and wearing worried faces, Clayton motioned to the right side of the entrance to the cave. "One minute please," he said as he began digging in the dirt. "I just have to look for something."

Clayton kept digging with his bare hands, deeper and deeper. "In my dream, I buried an arrowhead and bear tooth necklace here, right at this spot."

"I'll help you, man," Austin said as he and Daisy dug deeper.

"Clayton, I feel something! It feels pointy and slick," Austin said as he looked at Clayton with huge, bugged-out eyes.

Daisy continued to search in the dirt and out she pulled an arrowhead and eight teeth on a string of rawhide.

"THIS IS CRAZY!" Clayton screamed, as he patted Daisy. "This is just like the necklace in my dream that I buried to keep the tribe safe!"

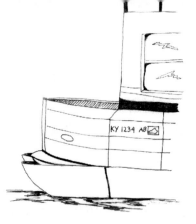

Chapter 10
Next Stop: Shaker Landing

As Clayton tied the necklace around his neck, Grampy, Mom, and Austin clapped and cheered for him.

"Maybe this will give us continuing good luck on our journey," Grampy joked. Next stop – Shaker Landing!

"And let's get lunch at Shaker Village," suggested Mom.

"Yes," answered Grampy, "And we only have a seven mile trip from here to Shaker Landing. Maybe you young men could research and take notes about Shaker Landing during our next hour of travel. The Kentucky River is very narrow through this area and we need to keep a steady watch for sand bars. My river map shows numerous sandbars between here and Lock 7."

"Alright, Grampy, we will take up our look-out posts

up at the bow. Clayton, do you want to survey the river for sandbars while I will examine the iPad?"

"Awesome! On it!" Clayton answered, as the boys took up their posts on the upper deck.

"I will watch from here on the main deck," Mom said. "Let's all try to keep glancing up because the beautiful high cliffs are still with us."

"No sight of any sandbars yet!" Clayton yelled down to Grampy and Mom after about 30 minutes.

"Hey, Clayton, let me tell you about Shaker Landing and Capt. James Harrod. He led an expedition of 37 men from Pennsylvania down the Ohio and Kentucky Rivers in 1774. Then they ditched their canoes and walked for about eight miles to a place where they found a spring. They built cabins there and they named the settlement Harrodstown. This was the first pioneer settlement in Kentucky.

"Man, I thought Boonesborough was," Clayton said.

"No, buddy, it was Harrodstown, later called Harrodsburg. The settlement grew with more and more pioneers coming from the east and they needed a fort for protection. Today, that fort is called Old Fort Harrod State Park.

"Now I remember," Clayton concluded. I went there on a field trip when I was what, in second grade? And I climbed in that big old tree."

"Oh, yeah, man, that osage orange tree! It says here that is the largest osage orange tree in the United States. It was there when the fort was built in 1775 and it is still growing!"

"Hello up top," Grampy called to the boys. Would one of you like to call the Lockmaster at Lock 7 to obtain permission to use the lock?"

"Sure thing," Austin answered. "Go ahead Clayton. I'll watch for the sand bars."

Clayton climbed down the ladder to the main deck, and prepared to call on Channel 13 of the marine radio. But a loud noise and a jolt from below deck caused him to stop. 'WHAT WAS THAT?" he shouted.

"WHIRLING WATERS, STARBOARD SIDE!" Austin blurted out.

"SANDBAR!" yelled Clayton.

"I'll rev up the engines to try to get us unstuck," Grampy consoled.

Grampy continued to shift the gears to go forward and then backward so the *Granny Rose* could get off the sand.

"Will we need to call the marina up ahead at Shaker Landing for help?" asked Mom.

Just then, Clayton remembered his good luck necklace, giving it a pat.

The *Granny Rose* jerked and then they all heard the normal sound of the engines.

"Made it out, "Grampy announced. "Whew, I'll maneuver us out of this tight area."

Clayton gave his necklace another pat, bowed his head, then stood up straight, looked up at the stairs to heaven and gave a thumbs up.

"We're good to make the call to the Lockmaster now," Grampy said as he slowly glided the *Granny Rose* toward Lock 7.

After the call, Clayton reported they needed to place the bumpers on the port side to tie up to the lock wall.

"This lock will place us 20 ft. higher in the Kentucky River," Grampy said, as Clayton, Mom, and Austin prepared the boat for the lock.

Clayton couldn't resist the urge to touch his necklace again as Grampy made his way through the lock.

"Grampy, I know we have traveled through a bunch of locks on this river adventure, but I just noticed the Lockmaster looking at our stern and entering something on his iPhone," Austin said. "What is he doing?"

"He's entering our Kentucky boat registration

number and checking our license number to make sure we are up to date. He sends the information to Frankfort so the State of Kentucky will have a record of the number of vessels who use the locks."

"Oh, good." Clayton gave a big exhale. "I thought we might be in trouble for something."

"Not with that bear tooth necklace of yours!" Grampy laughed, pointing to Clayton's neck. "Now we will need to change the bumpers to the starboard side so we can pull into the Shaker Landing Marina."

"There's already a houseboat parked up ahead. We can navigate in behind it." Mom pointed to the familiar looking vessel.

"Mom, that's Camryn on that houseboat!" Clayton waved his arms excitedly and Daisy barked and ran in circles.

"Hello, Little White Dove!" Clayton called to her. "I can't wait to tell you about my dream."

Camryn and her grandparents waved back as Grampy pulled into the boat slip. Clayton, Austin, and Mom secured the *Granny Rose*'s ropes to the dock and Grampy turned off the engines.

"Let's go see Camryn and Rocco. Come on, girl," Clayton said as he attached Daisy's leash.

"So what name did you have for me?" Camryn asked as she was trying to hold onto Rocco's leash. "Did you say something about a dream?"

"You were Little White Dove in my dream and I was Running Bird. All of us were in the dream and everybody had Native American names," Clayton answered while gasping for breath. "And you won't believe what happened!"

Chapter 11
Vibes for Camryn

Camryn listened intently as Clayton told her about his dream.

"That necklace you're wearing was the one you found in the cave?" Camryn asked in a curious voice. "And it was just like the necklace in your dream?"

Camryn touched the necklace respectfully. "That is SO COOL!" she exclaimed. "You should write a book about the vibes coming from your necklace!" She continued to finger the teeth and the arrowhead of the necklace and rubbed them as if expecting her own vibes.

"Would you like to wear it for awhile?" Clayton offered.

"Would I? Oh yes! Let's see what vibes I can get." Camryn gently took the necklace from Clayton and placed it around her neck.

After all the "nice to meet you" introductions from Clayton's group and Camryn's grandparents, Mom suggested they all walk up the hill to the Shaker Village Restaurant.

"Sure, that sounds great," Camryn's Grandpa Logan answered. "The restaurant even has outdoor tables so they would allow Rocco and Daisy to stay with us. We all need our walking shoes because it is about a 30 minute walk from here – all uphill!"

"30 minute walk?" questioned Austin. "Plenty of time for me to tell everyone about my research about Shaker Landing and the history of the Shakers," he said proudly.

"Sounds like a good plan," Grandma Lilly nodded. "I have been here before but I could use a refresher course about the Shakers."

As the group headed up the hill, Austin began sharing about Shaker Village. It was about 4,000 acres when the area was first settled at Pleasant Hill in Mercer County, Kentucky in 1805 by a group of religious people. They originally came from England to America in hopes of finding a Utopia. They traveled on foot from New York through the Cumberland Gap.

"So they wanted a perfect place to live?" Clayton

asked.

"Yes, but the community only lasted about 100 years. While they were here, they worked very hard at farming and making furniture from the multiple types of trees in the plentiful woods. They would load wagons and get them to Shaker Landing on the Kentucky River, where they shipped the products by flatboats down the Kentucky River to Carrollton.

"Yes, we've been there!" Clayton added. "They probably sent the products on the Ohio River to the north to Pittsburgh and south all the way to New Orleans, right?"

"Sure thing," Austin agreed. "Their sleek and non-decorative style of furniture is still very popular today. And guess what else they did? Built buildings and fences from stone! Imagine that! With rock from the Palisades!"

"Good research, Austin," Mom said. "I remember reading a book about the Shakers and they were far ahead in accomplishments than other settlers. They built a water system, an elevator at their mill, and they even had pumps in their kitchens."

"Not so bad for the 1800's," remarked Grandma Lilly. "Austin, did you learn what happened to their community, why it only lasted 100 years?"

"Apparently the older people began dying off and

the young people chose not to follow the strict guidelines of their religion. Everyone started moving on and heading further west," Austin answered. "But fortunately a group of Lexington, Kentucky citizens started the restoration of the Shaker Village in 1961, so, people can still tour the buildings and learn about their ways."

"Yeh!" Clayton shouted. "Look over there, top of the hill, the buildings. Boy, I'm glad we are almost there, I'm starved, especially after this uphill climb."

"Looks like we need to climb the fence ahead, cross that field, and then climb another fence," Grampy said, out of breath.

"Are there any animals in that field?" Camryn asked. "I think I see some big piles of doo-doo."

"Don't see any animals," answered Clayton. "We just have to be careful not to step in the...well, you know, the manure."

The group crossed over the fence and maneuvered Rocco and Daisy through the rails. As they dodged the piles and headed toward the other fence, the dogs suddenly stopped, not wanting to go another step. They began barking loudly. Even the gentle nudging from Clayton and Camryn didn't make the dogs budge.

Just then Camryn turned around and promptly

froze in place. "I think we need to get out of here, like, real quick," she whispered.

As they all turned around and saw the huge, black cow headed their way, their eyes bulged out and their mouths flew open.

"Okay, crew, we are not very far from the fence," Grandpa Logan said quietly. "No sudden moves, just slowly and steadily, we will walk to the fence. Clayton and Camryn, pet the dogs to let them know we are all okay here. When we get to the fence, Clayton and Camryn, you pick up the dogs and push them through the rails while the rest of us climb over as quickly as possible. Ready? One, two, three, slow and steady."

The dogs stopped barking and the group held hands proceeding through the field.

"Maybe I should look slowly behind us to see if the cow is charging," Clayton suggested. "Well...maybe not, let's just keep going."

It seemed an eternity, but the group finally reached the fence, Clayton picked up Daisy and Camryn picked up Rocco.

"Okay, we're here. Everybody know what to do next?" Grampy asked.

"Yes, ready, set, go!" Clayton bellowed.

"Wow, that was close," said Mom on the other side, as she saw Clayton, Daisy, Austin, Grampy, Grandpa Logan, and Grandma Lilly also on the other side.

"Camryn, what's wrong?" Clayton yelled, realizing she and Rocco were not to safety yet.

"The leash is stuck on this rail!" she called back.

"Camryn, touch the necklace!" Clayton hollered.

Hoping the vibes were coming her way, Camryn felt the teeth and arrowhead. Right on time, it seemed, she was able to unwrap the leash from the splinters in the decayed fence and pushed Rocco to safety. Then she climbed over the fence with lightning speed, hugging her grandparents and Rocco. By that time, the cow had arrived at the fence. It didn't try to get over the fence - just stuck its head under the bottom rail to get that tall, green grass. It raised its head and showed its teeth and mouth with the grass hanging out, as if to say, "It's okay. I just wanted some greener grass from the other side."

"Everybody alright?" Mom asked.

"Yes," Grampy answered, "must be that necklace of Clayton's, right?"

SHAKER
VILLAGE
★ ★ PASS ★ ★

— Chapter 12 —
Vibes Save the Day
at the Restaurant

"Hey, Clayton, maybe I should give this necklace back to you now," Camryn said as she reverently removed the necklace and placed it around Clayton's neck. "Thanks for the vibes."

Camryn was swaying back and forth and slid down in the grass, putting her face in her hands.

"Wow, I'm not ashamed to say it – that was majorly SCARY!" Camryn said softly. "I'll catch my breath here in a minute or two."

"Just look at the cow – still trying to get its head under the rail to get more grass," Clayton said as he gave the cow a mean looking face. "Remember that saying about the grass being greener on the other side of the fence? It must have come from a farmer watching his herd of cows."

Everyone shared a laugh and Camryn appeared to be feeling better.

"You, Mr. Cow, sure hope you enjoy your nice, fresh, green grass, but you scared the pa-toody out of me!" Camryn shook her fist at him.

"Everyone okay now?" Grampy asked. "Let's walk over to that Shaker Village map and locate the restaurant." Grampy motioned toward the sign.

"And to the restrooms!" remarked Camryn.

"Probably a needed thing for all of us," Austin added.

After the restroom and water fountain breaks, Clayton and Grampy searched the map.

"Here it is," Clayton said. Restaurant – end of this street! Follow me!"

As the group walked down the main street, they passed several interesting looking buildings – broom making, canned vegetables, jellies and jams, bake shop, weaving, animal barns, wagon rides, and the meeting house. There was even a sign that read: "Follow this trail to the stables."

"Looks like a lot to keep us busy this afternoon," Mom commented.

They approached the outdoor restaurant entrance

when an amusing thought hit Clayton, as he remembered the cheeseburger with no top at a Cincinnati restaurant.

"Do you think they have cheeseburgers here? I mean, with a bun on the top?"

Clayton then explained his experience to Camryn and her grandparents where he ordered a cheeseburger at a restaurant and it came out with no bun top.

"Well, Clayton, I think they have a flat-iron burger here," Grandpa Logan offered. "At least, they did the last time I was here."

"What? A flat-iron burger?" Clayton grimaced. "Does that mean the burger comes out really flat – like a pancake?"

"Maybe it's decorated with an iron on top and on a plate that is shaped like an ironing board," Austin said as he pretended to be ironing.

"Maybe it's just really skinny and comes out wrapped around – like – a curling iron!" Camryn made little curls with her fingers.

"Okay, you comedians," Grandma Lilly chuckled. "A flat-iron burger would be meat ground up from flat-iron steak. Usually the meat is prepared medium to rare in a cast iron skillet."

"Sounds good – let's go," Clayton said motioning for

everyone to hurry up.

The group took their places at one of the outdoor tables conveniently located among huge trees. They decided they would all order flat-iron burgers, even for Rocco and Daisy – only meat for them, of course.

"Hey, Clayton, did you notice all the sandwiches on the menu are the same price? What's up with that?" Austin asked.

"Interesting," Clayton responded. "Hey, look at all these people wearing Shaker Village ID lanyards. Some people have red ones and some have blue. Everyone has one except us."

"I just noticed that myself," Grampy answered in a concerned voice.

When the waitress came to take the food and drink orders, Grampy inquired, "Ma'am, what are those Shaker Village lanyards for?"

"I was just getting ready to ask you and your group where yours were? Each of you were supposed to get one at the ticket window. You pay to enter the grounds and tour all the buildings – that's red. If you pay extra for the restaurant, you get blue.

"That explains it!" Clayton poked Austin. "Food the same price and the red and blue ID's."

"Oh dear, so sorry. We didn't pay." Mom looked as if she was going to cry. "We walked up the hill from our boats docked at the Shaker Landing."

"You walked all the way up that hill?" the waitress inquired. "You must be one tired group of people – that hill is a monster! Plus, you have to cross through the angus cattle field."

"Oh, yeah!" everyone said in unison.

"We know all about the cow field, had an up close and personal experience with a monster cow," Camryn said, opening her hands and arms to show just how wide and tall that cow was.

"OH, NO, NO, NO!" The waitress first looked mortified, changed her expression to a slight smile, and finally to a wide grin. "Glad you made it! There's a ticket window at the main Shaker Village entrance. It's back down that way. You must've missed it."

Clayton's stomach began growling. It seemed to be saying, "feed me." He rubbed his stomach and then touched his necklace.

"We are so embarrassed," Grandpa Logan said. "Things have changed since I was here last."

"Don't worry, I'll bring your drinks and food ASAP. Can't have customers passing out from dehydration and starvation. You can pay later."

"Thank you, thank you," Grampy said while wiping his forehead.

"Clayton, did you just get some vibes from your necklace?" Camryn seemed to read the relaxed expression on his face as it changed from a worried look.

"OH, YES, SERIOUSLY YES! The vibes saved the day here at the restaurant."

Clayton exclaimed, while everyone except Camryn just shook their heads and showed disbelief on their faces.

Chapter 13
We're Not Walking Back!

"Grampy, the flat-iron burger tastes really good and it's not flat, it's thick!" Clayton laughed.

"Yes, and Daisy and Rocco seem to be enjoying their burgers too," Camryn noticed.

After everyone finished lunch, Grampy pointed down the street to the ticket booth. "We'd better go pay, so we're legal. Then, we can tour the buildings. I really want to see the blacksmith shop and some of us might want to take a wagon ride."

"I'm sure Clayton, Austin, and Camryn will enjoy seeing the dormitories," Mom said.

"What are dormitories?" Austin inquired.

"Large rooms with beds for as many as 25 to 40 people, and they are divided – boys in one and girls in another," Mom explained.

"Wow," Camryn rolled her eyes. "That's way too many people in one room, even if the room is big."

"I guess they could have a big party," Clayton added.

"Well...maybe not. Remember the Shakers were a very strict religious community," Grandpa Logan said.

After everyone paid the appropriate entrance fee and obtained their lanyards, the group headed out to enjoy the Shaker Village grounds and learn new things.

"Look at all the men and ladies in the shops. They are dressed in period costumes," Grandma Lilly mentioned.

"I know they believed in simpleness and dark colors," Austin offered but I read that sometimes they sewed a bright colored fabric on the inside of their clothes."

"Interesting, but I imagine their clothes made them extra hot, working outside in the summers," Mom surmised.

"Grampy, there's the sign for the stables, do you want to go there?" Clayton asked.

"Not sure I want to ride a horse, but you young gentlemen and lady might like to do that," Grampy said. "Let's split up and we can all meet back in one hour in front of the General Store."

"Got it!" Clayton answered as everyone coordinated

the time on their watches.

As Clayton, Austin and Camryn headed toward the stables, Grampy, Mom, Grandma Lilly and Grandpa Logan entered the "meeting house." There was a gentleman in period costume explaining that the Shakers began with a group of nine people from England who came to America for religious freedom. Their leader was a woman named Mother Ann. Ultimately, the community continued to gain members and 21 villages were established from Maine to Kentucky. They became known as "Shakers" because they participated in joyful movements in their worship. Only one community still exists today – in Maine.

"Let's go see how they made their brooms," Mom suggested.

After the demonstration in the broom-making shop, the group decided the brooms were very well made. "I am glad I can purchase one, and not have to make one like they did years ago," Grampy said.

"Oh yes, it's an easier lifestyle now in some ways," Mom agreed.

"I definitely want to get some of the homemade jam and jellies, along with the fresh bread," Grandma Lilly said as they toured a replica of a Shaker house and kitchen.

Grampy and Grandpa Logan were particularly

interested in all the tools in the blacksmith's shop. "Can you imagine being dressed in those dark, long sleeved clothes and standing over a fire on hot days to produce horseshoes, cooking utensils and farm implements!" Grampy marveled.

The hour flew by and everyone met at the General Store, some of the group purchasing crafts, brooms, jams, jellies, and fresh vegetables. Everyone compared notes about what they had seen and done.

"Grampy, look at that sign, 'trout fishing licenses available.' Do you think we could do that sometime tomorrow on our way to Boonesborough?" Clayton had those big eyes and intriguing smile on his face.

"We could PROBABLY do that," Grampy answered, with a little grin on his face.

"Awesome!" Austin exclaimed. "Probably means a 'yes,' right?"

"Sure, let's go for it! I know there is trout fishing in the Dix River. It runs into the Kentucky River not too far ahead. Let's talk to the lady at the counter about trout licenses."

"Are you going to fish with us tomorrow?" Clayton asked Camryn and her grandparents.

"No, we need to move on down the river to

Boonesborough. We will meet my parents there," Camryn replied. "Can't wait to see them and tell them all about Mr. Cow."

"May I help you?" the lady at the fishing license counter asked.

"Yes, ma'am, we need trout fishing licenses for four people for tomorrow," Grampy said. "And by the way, what kind of bait should we use?"

"Do you have any corn?" she asked.

"Corn, like in canned corn?" Clayton asked.

"Yes, absolutely! You put a few kernels of corn on your hook and the trout will come! Of course, you can use all the usual things, like worms and lures. Even balls of cheese will work."

"We have canned corn and cheese onboard the *Granny Rose*," Mom offered.

"Remember, there is a five trout per person limit," the saleslady said, ringing up the fishing licenses' payment.

"Thanks for your help," Austin told the lady, as he pretended he was casting in the water with his fishing pole.

"Let's head back to our boats now," Grampy motioned to the door.

"WE'RE NOT WALKING BACK!" he heard in unison from everyone.

"No takers to walk? Downhill is always easier that uphill," Grampy beamed.

"WE'RE NOT WALKING BACK!" he heard again, even louder than before.

"And we really don't want to see Mr. Cow!" Camryn pleaded.

"Sir, are you docked at Shaker Landing?" the saleslady asked.

"OH YES!" Clayton, Austin, and Camryn all answered together.

"I have a suggestion if you are interested. The plumbers have a van out back and they are getting ready to head down to Shaker Landing. They could probably give you a ride."

"Sounds like fun!" Austin announced.

As the saleslady introduced the group to the plumbers and they headed out the back door, the driver cautioned, "You are welcome to ride – well, with the damaged toilets and pipes!"

Everyone took their places in the van and began the trek down the hill on the road to Shaker Landing.

"Hang on back there!" the plumbers yelled.

"Mom, do you have your phone or iPad?" Clayton inquired. "Can you take a picture of us with these 'thrones'?"

After some crazy picture taking and a bumpy, noisy ride down the hill to Shaker Landing, Clayton's group and Camryn's group exchanged phone numbers and email addresses.

"Let's meet up again for another adventure!" Grampy suggested.

"Great idea!" Grandma Lilly agreed.

"We'll be traveling down the Ohio to the Mississippi River to Mobile and the Gulf Coast later this year," Grandpa Logan said. "Maybe you could join us somewhere in Alabama or the Florida panhandle. We will be docking in Destin, Florida for the winter months."

"Yes! And guess what? My parents and I are flying down to Destin for Fall Break and meeting Grandma and Grandpa there," Camryn said excitedly. "No telling what kind of adventures we could have on the beach, but NO COWS!"

"And hopefully no rides in a plumber's van!" Clayton said.

Chapter 14
Corn and Cheese Balls

"Mom, we have more cans of corn, right?" Clayton asked as he, Austin, and Daisy bounced up the steps from their bunks the next morning.

"Yes, I know we had corn at dinner last night, but, yes, we have more corn," Mom assured the boys.

"And cheese?" Austin inquired.

"Same thing, fellows, plenty of cheese left from last night also," Mom explained.

"Wow, you young men are already out of bed?" Grampy laughed.

"Yes, big day ahead, the trout await us," Clayton said, pretending he was reeling in a big, heavy fish.

"That sure is an interesting looking paddlewheeler docked down the way from us," Austin said, pointing to the

Dixie Belle.

"Yes," Grampy agreed. "It's propelled by a paddle wheel, whereas the *Granny Rose* has driveshafts and propellers moving us along. The Dixie Belle is a tour boat for anyone who wants to admire the Palisades and travel under High Bridge."

"We'll be passing under High Bridge this morning," Mom added. "It's a railroad bridge built in the late 1800's, quite a marvel for that day and time. It was the tallest railroad bridge in the world until the early 1900's."

"Okay, finish up that cereal and milk, deckhands, let's get ready to head out," Grampy encouraged.

"Grampy, will we be able to ride the wakeboards?" Clayton asked.

"Probably later today, right now we are not very far from the Dix River where we will be fishing," Grampy answered. "Guys, you could sit on the swim platform at the back of the boat. Mom and I can handle look-out posts at the front. My river map shows this is a very narrow section of waters we are entering, both the Kentucky and Dix. We will be traveling at a slower speed than usual."

"And I thought our normal 10 miles an hour seemed slow," Clayton grimaced.

"Okay, ropes ready, pumps ready, engines started,"

Grampy called as he maneuvered the *Granny Rose* out of its dock and into the Kentucky.

"High Bridge straight ahead," Mom announced.

"Awesome, look at how high that bridge is," Clayton marveled. "I can't imagine being a train conductor on that bridge."

"Sorry, I don't think I can look up," Austin bowed his head and closed his eyes.

"Oh, yeah, man, are you getting dizzy?" Clayton asked.

"Affirmative, friend, just like when I looked up at that high church steeple in Cincinnati. Totally EMBARRASSING!"

"Hey, no problem, buddy, remember I got dizzy looking down on the Ohio from the railing of the Purple People Bridge in Cincy," encouraged Clayton.

"Most people have some kind of phobia." Mom also wanted to encourage Austin. "Remember I'm the one who doesn't like snakes. Plus, I chickened out and wouldn't even walk on the Shark Bridge at the Newport Aquarium."

As they rolled on down the river, the boys sat on the swim platform and took off their socks and shoes and dangled their feet in the water.

"Dix River ahead, turning right," Grampy called.

"Trout, are you listening? We are on our way to get you."

"Clayton, my feet are getting cold, how about you?" Austin scooted back and retrieved his socks and shoes.

"Me too!" Clayton shouted as he put on his socks and shoes. "Grampy, our feet are...like...freezing! What's happening?"

"Trout live in cold water, about 55 degrees," Grampy said, pretending he was shivering. The water here in the Dix drains from the lower levels of Herrington Lake where the water stays cold. This is one of the few places in Kentucky where trout can survive. The Dix River Dam backs up water for flood control and for generating electricity as the water flows through turbines.

Grampy dropped anchor and the group unpacked all their fishing gear.

"Let's all be careful putting kernels of corn or cheese balls on our hooks," Mom cautioned.

"Mom and Grampy, how about you two using corn as bait, while Austin and I use cheese balls? We can have our own little fishing derby," Clayton suggested as he and Austin took cheese slices and formed them into balls.

"You're on, son," Mom agreed. She and Grampy prepared their hooks with corn kernels.

"Time limit – 30 minutes," Grampy said, looking at

his watch.

"Ready, set, cast! Game on!" Clayton announced.

"Grampy, why is there a limit on how many trout we can catch?" Austin asked as they all cast out their poles and watched eagerly for trout on the ends of their lines.

"These trout come from a hatchery. They are not native to the Dix," Grampy explained. "The Wolf Creek National Fish Hatchery is located at the Wolf Creek Dam south of Jamestown, Kentucky. It supplies cool water fish to other streams in Kentucky and even some other states.

"So how did the fish get here to the Dix?" Austin inquired.

"By truck, like a tanker truck," Grampy answered. "I remember I was driving on the highway here by the Dix several years back. I saw a fish truck backed up to the boat ramp. The trucker opened the valve and the fish swam right on out!"

At the end of the 30 minutes, Mom and Grampy had caught their limit of five trout each, while Clayton and Austin had caught three trout each.

"Okay, okay, okay, I suppose 'congratulations' are in order," Clayton said, patting Mom and Grampy on their backs.

"I, Chief Proud Foot, declare catching trout with corn

is FUN!" Grampy said, opening his arms down to the catch of fish laying in ice in the cooler.

"I will never look at a can of corn or cheese ball in the same way again," Austin declared.

The group readied themselves for the trip back down the Dix to the Kentucky. The boys decided to climb to the top deck and search on the iPad about Daniel Boone as Grampy successfully guided the *Granny Rose* through the narrow waters again.

"You might also search about Camp Nelson and the Perryville Battlefield," Mom suggested. "The river map shows we'll be passing by those areas on the way to Boonesborough."

"Yes, Ma'am," Austin laughed.

"But, Mom, with all these research assignments, what about some wakeboarding?" Clayton begged.

Chapter 15
It's on to Boonesborough!

After Grampy skillfully guided the *Granny Rose* back into the Kentucky River, the boys changed clothes and retrieved their wakeboards from storage.

"Man, are you wearing your necklace in the water?" Austin asked Clayton.

"Sure," Clayton said, smiling as he touched the necklace. "You know what – I did have another dream last night – about the necklace!"

"And...?" Austin quizzed.

"The dream was about Daniel Boone. He was leading some men through the woods and they were clearing a road for more settlers to come to Ft. Boonesborough AND HE WAS WEARING A NECKLACE LIKE MINE, with bear teeth and all!"

"Maybe you can find a special place for it in Boonesborough or you could keep it, of course," suggested Grampy.

"Good idea, there is a museum there," said Mom. "We could check it out."

"Very good," Clayton said with a thumbs up. "I'll think on it."

Daisy settled into her resting place while the boys enjoyed wakeboarding.

After their skin was about all shriveled up from an hour in the water, the boys gave a thumbs down signal to Mom that they were ready to pull up their ropes and boards.

"Mom, guess what?" Clayton said as he and Austin climbed back onto the swim platform and dried off.

"Now, let me see…" Mom said placing her hand on her chin as if in complete thought. "You two are hungry?"

"How'd you know that?" Clayton asked, shaking his head. "You always seem to know what I'm thinking."

"Moms know everything!" announced Austin.

"Now a question for you two," Mom said. "Ham or turkey sandwiches?"

As the boys helped with the lunches, Grampy reminded them about passing by Camp Nelson on the

Kentucky River.

"I did my research about Camp Nelson before we rode the wakeboards," Clayton boasted. "Camp Nelson was a Union fort in the Civil War used for storing supplies and training new soldiers. That camp provided over 10,000 trained men for the Union. There was even a refugee camp there for displaced families. It was named after Major General Bull Nelson. There is the Civil War Heritage Park there today."

"Okay, and I had time to research Perryville Battlefield before we did the wakeboarding," Austin gave himself a pat on the back. "Here goes: The Perryville Battle, located in Boyle County not far from here, was fought in 1862. It was the largest Civil War battle fought in Kentucky. The State of Kentucky was officially neutral during the war, but Confederate General Braxton Bragg launched an invasion into Kentucky. He wanted to recruit volunteers for the Confederate Army as well as interrupt Union movements in the South. Bragg eventually withdrew from Kentucky and headed back to the South."

"Gosh, I hope you young men remember all you've learned on our river adventure," Grampy complimented. "We are almost to the end of this adventure. It's on to Boonesborough and then back home to Louisville."

"Any surprises?" Clayton joked.

"You never know," Grampy laughed. "On my river map, we'll be going around Devil's Elbow shortly. We were headed in a southerly direction, but now the river makes a northeast turn. The map cautions about a big sandbar, so let's all watch carefully for those swirling waters."

"Let's do this," Clayton yelled as the boys and Mom assumed their look-out posts.

"Wow," Mom pointed to the Palisades. "These bluffs are the highest we have seen yet."

After more intense attention at the look-out posts, the group triumphed over the sandbar and narrow waters.

"We can relax a little bit now," Grampy said, wiping his forehead.

The boys decided to go to the top deck and peruse through some more of their comic books they purchased at the Comic Con in Cincinnati. Meanwhile, Mom and Grampy were making several phone calls and they were talking very softly.

"Clayton, I sense something's up," Austin said, poking Clayton. "Your mom and Grampy have been on the phone talking really low and they are smiling like crazy. Look! Now they are like...trying to disguise their laughter."

"Very suspicious," Clayton agreed.

"Hey, deckhands," Grampy called as he put down the cell phone. "We're coming up on the Valley View Ferry. It carries auto traffic on KY 169 from Richmond, in Madison County, to Nicholasville, in Jessamine County. It is the oldest continuously operated business in Kentucky, from way back in 1785.

"Grampy, did you research about the Valley View Ferry?" Clayton asked.

"No, actually I had an up close and personal encounter with the ferryboat. When I was working as a medical instruments salesman, I had visited doctors at the hospital in Richmond and I needed to get to my next appointment with a doctor in Nicholasville. I saw on my map that KY 169 would take me directly to Nicholasville without getting back on Interstate 75. BAD IDEA! I came cruising around a corner in the road and right there – smack dab in front of me was the Kentucky River! The road was a little wet and I almost slid into the river. The ferryboat captain kept laughing as he took me and my car across to the other side."

"I hear tires screeching all the time – only a few cars have actually plunged into the river!" he told me.

As everyone was having a big "ha-ha" at Grampy's expense, they all waved to the ferryboat captain as they passed the ferryboat platform.

"I sure hope there is some Hall's "snappy cheese" on sale at the Coonskin Cap Festival tomorrow," Mom said while smacking her lips and smiling.

"What is 'snappy cheese'?" Austin asked.

"It's a spicy type of cheese," Mom answered. "It was developed by a man named Joe Allman over 50 years ago. Eventually, the recipe was acquired by the Hall family in the 1960's. Now there is a fine restaurant, "Halls-on-the-River" just down river from Boonesborough. We will pass by there very soon.

"So we really are getting close to our final destination?" Clayton asked with a sad look on his face.

"Oh, yes," Grampy answered. "We head home in two days."

"But as soon as we dock at the Boonesborough Marina, we'll dive into the cooler and prepare those trout for dinner," Mom added.

"All right!" Clayton and Austin shouted, giving high-fives all around.

Chapter 16
A Home for the Necklace

"SURPRISE!" Clayton and Austin heard a chorus of voices behind them as they prepared to sit down to their trout fry on the *Granny Rose*.

"Dad!" Clayton shouted. "Didn't know you'd be here!"

Mom, Dad, Grampy, and Clayton shared a big bear hug.

"Mom, Dad!" Austin yelled out as his parents walked up the dock to the *Granny Rose*. Hugs abounded all around!

"How did you know we were here at the Boonesborough Marina?" Clayton questioned.

Just then, Austin recalled the secretive phone calls from that afternoon by Clayton's mom and Grampy. "Wait a minute, Grampy, were you talking to my parents today?"

"Who, me?" Grampy said innocently.

"Oh, yeah, and were you talking and laughing with Dad?" Clayton looked at Mom with a twinkle in his eye.

"Are you talking to me?" Mom also tried to have that 'not guilty' look.

"Dad, meet Daisy," Clayton said, bending down to pat her. As Dad and Austin's family got the traditional licks from Daisy, Clayton spied three familiar looking people and a little black dog approaching the *Granny Rose*.

"Look!" shouted Clayton.

"Hey there, Little White Dove (Camryn), did Chief Proud Foot (Grampy) call you today?" Clayton waved to her and her grandparents.

"Sure thing!" Camryn answered. "I have some exciting news for you – it's about your necklace."

Daisy and Rocco participated in the usual doggie greetings of licks, smells, and wagging tails, while all the adults got introduced.

"Do you think you all could meet us in Destin, Florida during Fall Break this year?" Camryn inquired. "We could travel the ICW and the Big C."

"The IC what, the Big what? You'll have to clue us in," Clayton advised. "But first of all, what's the news about the necklace?"

"Grandpa Logan and Grandma Lilly and I toured the museum in Boonesborough today. I was talking to the curator, Judy, about your necklace. Would you believe she showed me a viewing case where there was a necklace from none other than –Daniel Boone, and it looked like yours. Judy wants to meet you and evaluate your necklace. You probably found a home for the necklace – right here in Boonesborough – if you want to donate it, of course! She said she would even give everyone in your group Coonskin Caps as gifts. You don't have to buy them, like everyone else at the festival does!"

"Are you kidding? That is AWE...SOME!" Clayton answered.

"And guess what else was in the viewing case?" Camryn was so excited she could barely continue. "A journal from DANIEL BOONE where he wrote about meeting a Shawnee tribe and its leader was CHIEF RUNNING BIRD." Camryn had to stop talking momentarily to take a deep breath. "And the chief gave Daniel Boone A BEAR TOOTH NECKLACE!"

Everyone looked at Clayton for his reaction. His eyes were bulging, his face was frozen, and his legs were shaky. "Wow," he said softly. Then, recovering from his amazement, "WOW!" he exclaimed. "I, Chief Running Bird, declare this river adventure was NOT JUST AWESOME, IT WAS TOTALLY AND ABSOLUTELY AWESOME!"

Clayton raised his hands to the heavens in thanks, and everyone surrounded him giving handshakes, high fives, and thumbs up.

"Camryn," Clayton said excitedly, "now tell me about Destin and this IC and Big C - whatever their names are. It sure sounds like more adventures to me!"

Nautical Language

Aft
The back section of a vessel.

Bow
The front side of a vessel.

Bridge
The place in the vessel where the controls are located.
(Example – steering wheel, gears, etc.)

Captain
The first person in command of a vessel.

Channel
That part of a waterway open to navigation.

Deckhand
A helper on a vessel.

Depth gauge
A device used to measure the distance from the bottom
of a vessel to the bottom of a waterway.

First mate
The second person in command of a vessel–
takes captain's place if necessary.

Flatboat
A boat with about 2-3-ft. sides all around, no point
in front, with a flat bottom.

Moorings
Ropes and any attachments that connect a vessel to a dock.

Mouth
The point where one waterway drains into another waterway.

Port
The left side of a vessel.

Starboard
The right side of a vessel.

Stern
The rear of a vessel.

Vessel
Any sized watercraft.

Wake
Waves given off by the movement of a vessel.

Wheelhouse
The area of vessel that contains the steering controls and gauges.

Special Resources for Parents, Grandparents and Teachers

To be used with Clayton's River Adventure Continues: The Dog Days of Summer

Reading

Before the reading:

1. Do you have a dog? If so, how does the dog act with you? If you don't have a dog, tell why or why not you would want a dog.

2. Have you ever been to a horse race or watched one on TV? If so, state your opinion of the race. If not, tell why you would or would not like to attend a horse race.

3. Have you ever been fishing? If so, tell about your enjoyment or not of fishing. If not, explain if you would be interested in going fishing or not.

4. Do you share your good dreams with anyone? What about the not-so-good dreams? Why or why not?

5. Tell about any object you have that seems to bring you good feelings.

During the Reading:

1. Why was Clayton allowed to keep Daisy?

2. What things were purchased for Daisy at the pet store?

3. Do you think Daisy was a smart dog? Cite examples from the book.

4. Why did Mom want to bring Sweikart Miss home with her?

5. Why did Grampy and his family cry when Sweikart Miss was claimed by a new owner?

6. Why do horses and cows need salt?

7. Why do you think Mr. Chapman gave Clayton and Austin a dreamcatcher?

8. In Clayton's dream, why did he bury the necklace?

9. Why do you think Grampy called the Palisades "Stairways to Heaven?"

10. What did the group find when they explored the cave at Shawnee Run?

11. Name the first pioneer settlement in Kentucky. Who was it named after?

12. List some of the accomplishments of the Shakers that were very advanced for that time in history.

13. Explain the decision by Clayton's group to ride in the plumber's van.

14. What did Camryn suggest for Clayton to do with the necklace?

After the Reading:

1. Evaluate the retirement years for horses.

2. Would you want to fillet fresh fish? Why or why not?

3. What might happen to the trout fishing industry in Kentucky if there was no limit on how many trout a person could catch?

4. If you were Clayton, would you give the necklace to the museum? Give your reasons.

Math

1. See the Math problem in Chapter 3 about how long it will take to get to Boonesborough.

2. See the Math problem in Chapter 4 about the percentage of horses making it into the Kentucky Derby.

3. Camryn's grandparents are planning a houseboat trip from Louisville down the Ohio and Mississippi Rivers and Intracoastal Waterway to Destin, Florida. Research about the number of miles for the trip. If they travel an average of 10 miles per hour, for 10 hours a day, how many days will their trip take?

Social Studies, Science, Writing

1. Research about the training of thoroughbred horses. Advise your parents on the pluses and negatives about owning race horses.

2. Research about different types of bait. What are the best choices for the fishing in the waters in your area? Share your findings with family or friends for their next fishing trip.

3. Research about Daniel Boone and Boonesborough. Write a letter to your teacher giving reasons why he or she should plan a field trip there for your class.

References

Chapman Piloting Seamanship and Boat Handling, Elbert S. Maloney, 63rd Edition, The Hearst Corporation, 1999.

"Expanded Hatchery Creek to open Friday," The Courier-Journal, Gary Garth, April 24, 2016.

"Hatchery Creek opens up options for trout anglers," The Courier-Journal, Gary Garth, May 8, 2016.

The Kentucky River, William E. Ellis, The University Press of Kentucky, 2000.

"KY tightens warnings on fish consumption," The Courier-Journal, James Bruggers, February 19, 2016.

"New law protects Kentucky's stray horses," The Courier-Journal, Lori Redmon, April 17, 2015.

The Ohio River, Tim McNeese, Chelsea House Publishers, 2004.

The Ohio River, John Ed Pearce, Photographs by Richard Nugent, The University Press of Kentucky, 1989.

Wikipedia

Http://bluegrasswoodland.com/uplaods/Palisades-Notes.pdf

Http://www.campnelson.org/home.htm

www.cumminsferry.com

Http://www.fortboonesboroughlivinghistory.org/html/
daniel-boone.html.

Http://www.frankfort.ky.gov/general-information/
frankfort-history

Http://www.hallsontheriver.com/about-us.html.

fw.ky.govKentucky Dept. of Fish and Wildlife Resources
Kentucky River, Pool6.

www.kyhumane.org.

www.kentuckyriverblueway.com

Http://www.uky.eduKentuckyRiverNavigationCharts

Http://www.newworldencyclopedia.org/entry/
Dreamcatcher

www.riverlorian.com

www.shakervillage.ky.org/history-and-restoration/

Http://shakervillageky.org/plan

Http://shakervillageky.org/the-river/

Clayton's Fast Facts

About the Ohio River

Runs 981 miles from Pittsburgh, Pennsylvania to Cairo, Illinois, where it flows into the Mississippi River.

In the 1500's, Native Americans apparently had a well developed civilization along the Ohio, which they called the "Beautiful River."

In the 1600's, French explorer, Sieur deLaSalle, reportedly explored the Ohio to the Falls at what is now Louisville and turned around. The next year, he explored all the way to the Gulf of Mexico.

In the 1700's, the French and English disputed over the river territory, and the English eventually drove the French out. A trading post for the early settlers was opened in Pittsburgh.

In 1778, George Rogers Clark led a group of settlers from Pittsburgh downriver to Louisville at the Falls. Riverboats could not navigate the 25 ft. drop in the water level.

In the 1800's, the Portland Canal was built around the Falls of the Ohio to allow riverboat traffic to continue beyond Louisville, providing better access to the Midwest at St. Louis and to the South at New Orleans.

In the 1900's, a system of locks and dams was built on the Ohio providing even easier access for riverboat traffic.

From the 1800's to today, the U.S. Army Corps of Engineers oversees the Ohio River.

Today, the Ohio River is home to approximately 120 species of fish, and a decreasing population of wildlife along the river.

About the Kentucky River

The Kentucky River flows from Beattyville, KY and empties into the Ohio River at Carrollton, KY. It runs in a northwestly direction for 255 miles. There is a drop of 226 feet in the water level from Beattyville to Carrollton.

Native American tribes were the first inhabitants along the KY River. They were attracted to the area because of abundant forests, wildlife, and fertile soil. It is reported that Gabriel Arthur may have been the first white man to see the KY River in 1674. Daniel Boone and other hunters came to the area in the 1700's. The Native Americans and the European settlers kept pushing further westward along natural trails.

The settlements along the Ohio River and KY River survived Native American attacks and the British in the Revolutionary War. As George Rogers Clark and his group gained more control of the land along the Ohio River, the KY River settlements from Beattyville to Carrollton also became more stable.

The KY River provided a waterway for settlers to move crops, animals, salt, logs, and other products to the Ohio River at Carrollton and from there, the products could be shipped north to Pittsburgh or south to Louisville, St. Louis, and New Orleans.

The invention of steamboats provided a new way for transporting goods on the KY and a series of locks and dams were built on the KY. In 1842 there were five locks from Frankfort to Carrollton. Railroads came to the area in the 1880's, changing the way goods were to be moved and rendering the KY useful for recreation purposes, but not the movement of goods.

The Civil War caused much damage to the dams and locks on the KY because both Northern and Southern troops wanted control over them. The whole river system was in disarray. Money from the U.S. Congress was used to rejuvenate the lock and dam system with nine more modern locks from Frankfort to Beattyville. In 1914, Lock #14 was finished at Beattyville.

Today, there is very little commercial traffic on the KY but has a generous amount of recreational use. The constant spring floods and summer droughts continue to be a problem for economic growth in the area.

About Dream-catchers

A dream-catcher began as a Native American object. It has a ring made of red willow, or similar pliable bark, and held together by a web of sinew or tough tissue. It connects to the ring in seven or eight places forming a web. There are several feathers at the base of the dream-catcher.

There is a theory that the dream-catcher originated with the Ojibwe tribe. It was first documented in 1929. As different Native American came together in the Pan-Indian Movement during the 1960's and 1970's, the tradition of the dream-catcher spread and became a symbol of unity among the various tribes.

Dream-catchers are used to encourage good dreams and pass through the hole in the middle of the web, while the bad dreams become trapped in the web and evaporate in the morning. In the Ojibwe tradition, dream-catchers were often made by grandparents and hung over an infant's cradle.

Today the popularity of dream-catchers has spread and they have become commercialized, found hanging in many places other than a child's nursery. Some Native Americans think dream-catchers are a harmless tradition, some think of them as tacky, while others see them as symbols of unity.

About the Author
Linda M. Penn

Linda M. Penn holds a master's degree and Rank I degree in Elementary Education from the University of Louisville. She taught kindergarten through third grade for twenty-one years in public schools.

Linda's first book, *"Is Kentucky in the Sky?"* won the Silver Medallion from Mom's Choice Awards. Her second book, *"Hunter and the Fast Car Trophy Race"* features a young boy who loves stock car racing. *"Clayton's Birding Adventure,"* her third book, features a youngster who moves to a new neighborhood and school and makes friends in an unusual way.

"No More French Fries in the Bed," features the returning characters of Allyson and Samantha, who overcome the feud over the messiness of their room. *"No Pink Glasses"* features the returning character of Hunter who is torn between fear and courage regarding his need for glasses.

"Clayton's River Adventure" and *"Clayton's River Adventure: Cincinnati to Frankfort,"* written with Linda's cousin, Frank Feger, brings Clayton and Austin back, this time returning in an adventure on the Ohio and Kentucky Rivers.

Linda's website and blog, **lindampenn.com** contains many resources geared for parents and teachers to enhance the reading experience with their young ones. You can read her blog about writing and reading for children and download the educational resources for free. To contact Linda, you can email her at lindampenn@gmail.com.

About the Author
Frank Joseph Feger

Frank was born in Louisville Ky., and graduated from St. Xavier High School and United Electronics Institute with a degree in Electronics. As a Vietnam era Veteran, he served three years in the U.S. Army.

Frank was a Medical Electronics Sale Representative for 40 years. He worked for Malkin Instrument Co. and sold pacemakers, defibrillators and cardiac monitors for 10 years. He worked for Olympus Medical Corp. for 30 years and sold gastrointestinal endoscopes in Kentucky, Indiana and Ohio. Frank retired in 2007 and is the VP of the Colon Cancer Prevention Project in Louisville, Ky.

Feger has been a boater for 55 years. The boat mentioned in the book, *The Granny Rose*, was a 42-foot Harbor Master Houseboat that made two trips to Cincinnati. Frank and his family enjoyed the boat and the trips all his family and friends embarked on.

At a family reunion, Linda and Frank met upon an interesting boating conversation. Linda had already been thinking about publishing another Clayton book, and upon hearing Frank's river traveling stories, the two decided to mesh their experiences together and embark on another Clayton adventure–this time down the Ohio and Kentucky Rivers.

About the Illustrator
Melissa Quinio

Melissa Noel Quinio went to the University of Louisville to study Fine Arts and Psychology. She now lives in Lexington, Ky with her four children (two boys and two girls) and her husband, Edward. She spends her time creating new and exciting works of art and spending precious time with her family.